BRUNO'S BAND

Benedict Blathwayt

WALKER BOOKS
LONDON

For Timmy and Joe

First published 1986 by Julia MacRae Books
This edition published 1992 by Walker Books Ltd
87 Vauxhall Walk, London SE11 5HJ

Printed and bound in Hong Kong by
Sheck Wah Tong Printing Press Ltd

British Library Cataloguing in Publication Data
A catalogue record for this title is available
from the British Library.

ISBN 0-7445-1373-1

Bruno was a restaurant cat. Carlo the cook and his wife Maria
loved Bruno; they made sure he never went hungry.
The restaurant was a happy place and Bruno was a happy cat.

The customers all loved him, too.
It was not only the delicious food they came for – they came to see Bruno. He was a special cat: when the moon rose and stars blinked in the evening sky, Bruno would take his fiddle and play soft and beautiful music under the old cork tree. This was his home. Bruno knew there was no better life than his.

But Carlo and Maria seemed to spend their whole life cooking and washing-up. "We really must have a holiday," said Maria one day. Bruno watched the excitement and muddle as they packed, but he did not understand what was happening.

TAXI

On the morning that Carlo and Maria
left, Bruno lay fast asleep in the warm grass.
He did not even hear them go. New people came to
look after the restaurant. No one had told them about Bruno;
in the rush and bustle of last minute preparations he had
been forgotten.

Again and again that day, the strangers chased him
from the kitchen. Did they think he was a stray?
Bruno was sad and bewildered.
What could he do?

VIKING
EMILY
EMILY

Bruno left the home he loved. He wandered through the town and down to the harbour. Here, the world seemed a strange and a lonely place. Bruno felt he belonged nowhere.

"You're welcome aboard," said the captain of a small steamer, "I could do with some company."

But once they were out at sea
Bruno knew he would never make
a good ship's cat; the waves
were too big and the salt spray
too cold.

The captain's parrot became Bruno's friend. Sometimes, when the wind whistled in the rigging and the sea was rough, they would play a shanty or a jig together. Then the voyage seemed not so long and Bruno felt a little less homesick. But the two friends secretly agreed that as soon as possible they would search for a better way of life.

At the next port, in the middle of the night, Bruno and the parrot quietly slipped ashore.

The city was huge and unfriendly. They walked all day, and had just given up hope of finding any place to rest when they were joined by a dog.

"I see you are musicians like me," said the dog, "I play the pipes. Follow me and you will come to no harm."

That night, around a warming fire, the animals made music.

"If we are going to stick together," said the dog, "then we must think of a way to earn food and shelter."

"A dog can find work in the country," said the parrot. "The country is the place to go!"

"There *must* be a better place than this," agreed Bruno. He was hungry, the shadows and night noises made him shiver.

Early the next morning they made their way to the station. They were not completely alone on the platform. “May I come with you?” asked the station cat. “I see you are a band of musicians, and I play the guitar.”

“Of course,” said Bruno, and he and his new friends made the station cat welcome.

WAITING ROOM
TICKETS

Together they wandered the sidings until the
station cat found them an empty wagon.
In no time at all, with a jolt and rusty squeaks, their
journey had begun.

The air in the country smelled sweet. The fields of summer wheat curled and whispered like the sea.

When the train stopped at a crossing, the animals climbed from the wagon and made their way to the nearest farm. Here the dog found work, but he was not very good at his job. Each day he grew more and more miserable at being so useless.

He shared with his friends the little food he had. Two of the farm geese joined Bruno's band. At night, when the autumn winds moaned outside the barn, they all played music together.

“But it’s no good,” said the parrot one cold evening, “we’ve all had enough. We’ll have to earn our keep somewhere else.”

Bruno agreed, “There must be a better way than this.”

So they gathered their instruments together and crept away from the frozen farm.

Through the winter, Bruno and his band travelled from town to town. They worked hard, but found no place they could call home. They played anywhere: in market squares and parks, on pavements and in front of shops. People stopped to listen. Into the guitar-case they threw nuts, biscuits, chocolate and fruit – it was their way of saying thank you to the animals for their music.

"This is going well!" Bruno whispered to his band. But he still felt that somewhere, somehow, there was an even better life.

Time passed, and then, one spring afternoon, something tugged at Bruno's heart. "I think I know this place," he said to his companions. Yes, the old smells and sounds really were here. "It is *my* town!"

They ran together down the hill and suddenly there was the restaurant. But everything seemed strangely neglected and sad. There were no customers, no cooking smells, no bustle, and no fuss.

Carlo could not believe it when he saw Bruno!

He opened his arms wide and hugged Bruno and each of his five friends. Then he told them how all his customers had given up coming when they realised Bruno was gone for ever. He and Maria had come back from holiday to find their business ruined by the cook who did not like cats.

That afternoon Carlo and Maria lit the stove and cleaned the tables, they scrubbed the shutters and put new coloured bulbs above the canopy. Posters went up all over town. BRUNO IS BACK, the notices said, BRUNO AND HIS BAND WILL PLAY TONIGHT.

Later that evening, Bruno and his band began to play. The music floated away over the town and people came out of their houses to listen. "Bruno is back," they said to each other, and they set off for Carlo and Maria's restaurant once more.

Bruno and his band played and played.

"There is no better life than this," said Bruno, "We don't need to travel any further. This is home!"